The Secret Life of Mr. Mugs

By:
Mary Ellen Adair
Noreen Hishon
Doreen Lackenbauer

Literature Consultant:
Janet Lunn

Consultants:
Carl Braun
Allan R. Neilsen

Editors:
Wanda Moore
Lou Arrell

Staff Artists:
Halina Below
Dale Kasarda

D1711997

Starting Points in Language Arts

GINN AND COMPANY
EDUCATIONAL PUBLISHERS

Starting Points in Language Arts

Level One: Mr. Mugs
               Mr. Mugs — A Jet-Pet

Level Two: Mr. Mugs Plays Ball
               Mr. Mugs And The Blue Whale

Level Three: First Prize For Mr. Mugs
               Mr. Mugs Is Lost

Level Four: Sharing Time
               Happy Days For Mr. Mugs
               In A Dark Wood

Level Five: Mr. Mugs At School
               In The Rain
               Mr. Mugs To The Rescue

Level Six: Mr. Mugs Is Kidnapped
                It's Saturday
                Feather Or Fur

Level Seven: Just Beyond
                What If?
                The Secret Life Of Mr. Mugs

ISBN: 0-7702-0259-4

Contents

The Secret Life of Mr. Mugs

One morning Mr. Mugs stretched himself and sat at the bottom of the stairs. Mr. Mugs had a rash on his neck and he wanted a special pat or a hug. When Mommy came downstairs she gave Mr. Mugs a pat on the head and said, "How's Mr. Mugs this morning?" There was something Mommy did not realize.

When Daddy came downstairs he looked at Mr. Mugs's neck and said, "Your rash is clearing up. Soon we can put your collar back on." There was something Daddy did not realize.

Jan and Curt gave Mr. Mugs a special hug and said, "Come, Mr. Mugs. Come to breakfast." Mr. Mugs didn't seem to be interested. There was something Jan and Curt did not realize.

After breakfast Mr. Mugs watched Tiger playing on the lawn with a catnip mouse. When school was over he ran after Jan's bicycle. But every night something happened that nobody knew about.

Every night Mr. Mugs would start across the backyard toward the doghouse, but he wouldn't go in. Instead, Mr. Mugs would trot down the street in the darkness until he was seven blocks from home. Then he would bound right up to a door where a light was shining. Every night the door would open and old Mr. Higgins would say, "Well, well, Jimpson John, it's about time you were getting home!" Then he would take Mr. Mugs inside.

First Mr. Higgins would give Mr. Mugs his dinner. Then he would sit down in his big chair with Mr. Mugs at his side and say, "Well, Jimpson John, what did you do today?" Later Mr. Mugs would close his eyes and sleep all night by the chair.

Early each morning Mr. Higgins would give Mr. Mugs a hearty breakfast and put him out before he went to work. Up the street Mr. Mugs would go until he reached home. Curt and Jan would let him in, and then Mr. Mugs would wait at the bottom of the stairs.

No one knew about Mr. Mugs's secret life.

One day after school when Mr. Mugs was chasing Jan's bicycle, he saw Tiger hiding in the bushes. Off he went after the cat — through the lumberyard, across the railroad tracks, behind some warehouses, and down the hill to the river.

This was the first time Mr. Mugs had been to the waterfront. Mr. Mugs was so excited that he hardly knew what to do first. He found a rat crouched near a warehouse and chased it four blocks. Then he

stood on the wharf and barked at boats. Next Mr. Mugs upset a fish barrel.

"Where's Mr. Mugs?" asked Mommy at dinner time.

"I don't know," replied Curt, feeling worried. "He was chasing Tiger the last time I saw him."

Six o'clock came, seven, and then eight . . .

Everyone became so worried that Mommy decided to call the police station. "Hello, Captain Maloney," she said, "we've lost Mr. Mugs. He's our sheep dog. He has a white head and chest and white paws. The rest of him is gray. His hair covers one eye."

"Okay," said Captain Maloney. "We'll call you if we find him."

Seven blocks away Mr. Higgins said to himself, "Can't understand it. Jimpson John has always been home before this."

He went to the phone and called the police. "I want to report a lost sheep dog," he said. "His name is Jimpson John. He has a white head and chest and white paws. The rest of him is gray. His hair covers one eye."

"Okay, we'll call you if we find him," said Captain Maloney. "Hmmm," he said to himself as he hung up. "Two sheep dogs lost in one night . . ."

At ten o'clock Mr. Mugs was still down by the river. He wasn't happy. His bones ached. He was so tired that he couldn't even find his way home.

Suddenly Mr. Mugs looked up. There on the bank of the river was a police car. Mr. Mugs knew that police cars meant "help" and right away he felt better.

The police officer took Mr. Mugs to the police station. Captain Maloney didn't know whether the dog was Mr. Mugs or Jimpson John. He reported the "found" dog to both families.

Mr. Higgins reached the station first. When Mr. Mugs saw him, he jumped down from the captain's desk and licked the old man on the cheek.

"It's Jimpson John, all right," said Mr. Higgins.

Mr. Higgins was just coming out of the station with Jimpson John when Jan, Curt, Mommy, and Daddy drove up.

"That man has Mr. Mugs!" cried Jan.

When Mr. Mugs saw Jan and Curt he felt playful again. He jerked loose and raced down the sidewalk with Mr. Higgins after him. Jan ran after Mr. Higgins; the rest of the family ran after Jan. Captain Maloney came running out of the police station when he heard the excitement.

If there hadn't been a fire hydrant on the corner, who knows how much farther Mr. Mugs would have gone? When he stopped to sniff, Mr. Higgins grabbed him. Jan tried to grab him at the same time.

"He's my dog!" cried Mr. Higgins, pulling on Mr. Mugs's hind legs. "He's slept at my house for over two weeks now!"

"No, he's our dog!" shouted Jan.

"How can one dog be two dogs?" wondered Captain Maloney.

"Mr. Mugs belongs to Jan and Curt," explained Daddy. "He usually wears a name tag but right now he has a rash and can't wear his collar. See?" Daddy showed Captain Maloney the rash on Mr. Mugs's neck.

"Hmmm," said Captain Maloney. "What does your dog do during the day, Mr. Higgins?"

"I suppose he plays with the neighborhood children," said Mr. Higgins rather doubtfully.

"And what does your dog do at night?" the captain asked Daddy.

13

"He sleeps in the doghouse in the backyard — I think," said Daddy.

"Well, it looks as if this dog has been living a secret life!" exclaimed Captain Maloney. "He's been getting four meals a day and living at two houses. But since he seems to be Curt and Jan's dog, Mr. Higgins, I guess you'll have to give him back."

Mr. Higgins sat down on the curb and hugged Jimpson John. "I'm going to miss you," he said sadly.

Jan thought for a moment and then said, "Mr. Higgins, I could bring Mr. Mugs over to visit you."

Mr. Higgins smiled. "That's very kind of you, Jan," he said. "I'd like that very much. Would it be all right if I call him Jimpson John when he comes?"

As Jan nodded her head, Mr. Mugs wagged his tail . . . he liked the idea too. He even seemed to have a smile on his face.

"The Secret Life of Mr. Mugs" is another story that you could make into a play. If you need some help in preparing for it, read "Making a Play" in the book *Mr. Mugs is Kidnapped*.

Slippery Slide

The slippery slide is very steep,
Up the high ladder you have to creep;
Sit down and take hold
       and give a little push.
Down you go with a swish and a swoosh!
Down you go with a swoosh and a slide,
Down the slippery slide
       you have a quick ride.
Jump off at the bottom,
       around you run,
Up the ladder again
       to have some more fun;
Sit down in your place
       and give a little push —
Down you go with a swish and a swoosh.
Down the slippery, slippery, slippery slide,
Oh, what fun it is to ride!

Lois Lenski

15

The Quitting Deal

Mommy said she'd quit if I quit. She wants me to quit sucking my thumb, because I'm getting too big for such baby stuff, she says. And the dentist says my new teeth might not come in straight if I keep sucking my thumb so much. Daddy and I want her to quit smoking, because the doctor says it's terrible for you, and she does cough an awful lot. I won't mention the hole she burned in the sofa cushion and the ashes she keeps dropping on my baby brother's head when she's feeding him. So we made a deal. We'd quit together.

The Holding Hands Cure

The first thing we decided was that we had to help each other. So we made a sticking-together plan. Whenever Mommy felt like smoking a cigarette, she'd come to me and I'd hold both her hands. Tight. And whenever I felt like sucking my thumb, we'd do the same thing, only opposite.

We did a lot of tight holding that first day. It was okay for a while, but then I needed my two hands back to finish this block city I was making. Anyway, Mommy needed her hands loose for cooking dinner. That was okay, too, because we were so busy for an hour we forgot all about wanting cigarettes and thumbs. Except later we remembered again.

The Candy Cure

When I got up the next morning, Mommy was sitting at the kitchen table with her cigarettes and matches in front of her. She wasn't smoking, but she looked awfully sad. When I asked her what was the matter, she said, "I miss having something in my mouth. Maybe I should start sucking my thumb."

"Mommies can't suck their thumbs!" I yelled. But then I had an idea. I took my allowance money. "You wait there," I called to Mommy. "No smoking. I'll be right back." And I ran around the corner to the candy store and bought a big bag of sucking candies. "Here," I said, and I dumped a whole mountain of them out in front of her.

First Mommy sucked a red one and then she sucked an orange one. Pretty soon she began to look

happier. Then she noticed I wasn't looking so great. "I guess you need something in your mouth, too," she said, and passed me a purple one.

That day we ate 106 sucking candies and all we had left were nine green ones, and we were even starting on those when Mommy jumped up and said, "This is terrible. Sure, I'm not smoking and you're not sucking your thumb, but we're going to get millions of cavities from all this candy, and then where will we both be?"

I couldn't answer that.

"Save the green ones for your daddy," she said. "He likes them."

The Comforting Cure

For me the worst time was going to sleep at night. Mommy said, "I'll come and sit by your bed." So I put on my pink cat pajamas and she came in and read me a story. Then she put out the light and sang me five songs. And then she just sat there, you know, to comfort me. And I got wider and wider awake. It wasn't working. So finally I told her, "I need my thumb, Mommy, not you." For going to sleep I had to have my thumb, and that was that.

She understood and went into the living room and smoked a cigarette.

The Penny Cure

"Every time you suck your thumb," Daddy said to me, "you have to put a penny into this box." Then he said to Mommy, "Judy, you have to pay a nickel for every cigarette you smoke. Into this box, right?"

"Why do I have to pay more?" Mommy asked. I think she was beginning to be sorry she had asked Daddy to help.

"Because you're richer. Jennifer's allowance is only fifty cents a week."

"What are you going to do with all our money, Daddy?"

"It's not for me. At the end of the week I'll take it out and send it to the poor children."

At the end of the week I was the poorest child I knew.

Mommy was smoking a whole pack of cigarettes a day. "I can afford it," she said.

"Judy," Daddy said, "you are a rich and foolish woman. As for you, Jennifer, you are simply foolish."

He sent Mommy's seven dollars and my twenty-six cents to the poor children and said, "Judith, I think you and your daughter will have to solve this problem on your own."

"Don't call me Judith," Mommy said.

The Food Cure

For Mommy the worst thing about not smoking was getting fat. She didn't mind not smoking at all, she said, as long as she could be eating. So whenever she felt like smoking she ate something instead. And all the tangerines and crackers and peanuts and chicken wings and heels of bread and chocolate bars just stuck there and by the end of two weeks there were eight extra pounds of her. But at least she wasn't coughing any more.

"I feel like a new woman," she said. "A new fat woman."

I thought she looked nice. Cosy, like a hamburger bun, but her clothes didn't fit and she couldn't buy a lot of new ones. She was saving her money in case I was going to need braces on my teeth after all.

So she went on a diet. For the next two weeks she didn't eat much or smoke much or smile much. At the end of the two weeks Daddy said, "Judy, now you are thin and healthy and very mean. But I love you anyway." And he told us his new plan.

The Next-to-Last Cure

If I stopped thumbsucking and Mommy stopped smoking, we'd each get a reward of what we wanted most.

Mommy wanted breakfast in bed every Sunday, forever. I wanted ballet lessons.

We reminded each other, whenever we wanted thumbs and cigarettes.

"Pink slippers," she'd say to me.

"Cinnamon toast," I told her.

But sometimes when I was alone in my room, all I could think about was my thumb. I'd get a strange, bad, twitchy feeling near my stomach. It felt like a mean little rabbit gnawing away at my insides, and then I just had to suck my thumb. I guess Mommy knew that rabbit, too, because the next afternoon Daddy came home and found her smoking again.

"Judy," he yelled. "What about your reward?"

"It's just not worth it," Mommy said. "Besides, you make terrible coffee."

Daddy said I could have the ballet lessons if I helped him make Mommy's Sunday breakfasts.

Mommy hugged him and said, "That's the trouble with you, George. You can't stick to anything."

"Just like some people I could name," Daddy said, but he didn't name us.

"You know, Jennifer," Mommy said suddenly, "this is ridiculous. I am a grown woman and you are a grown girl of eight. So we must stop being silly. We must just decide to quit. And then quit. No more smoking for me and no more thumbsucking for you. Ever again. Period."

"Mommy," I said, "I can't."

"I know, Jenny," she said. "I can't either."

Finally we decided she wouldn't stop smoking altogether, and I wouldn't stop sucking my thumb all at once. We'd just do it a little bit less. We'd kind of sneak up on quitting a little bit at a time. So far it's working. It does help when you've got someone to keep you company.

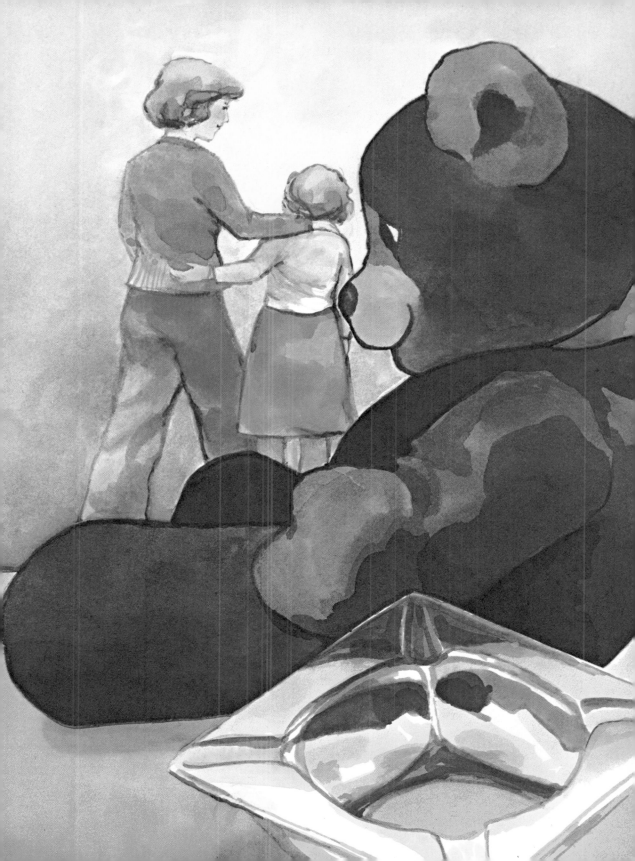

What Do You Do When . . . ? Teacher-Read

"Hi Scott! Do you want to skip stones?" asked Anthony.

"You can't skip stones here. There's no water anywhere," said Scott. "Besides, you heard Mrs. White yesterday when she said we weren't supposed to throw stones on the playground. Somebody could get hurt."

"I'm not going to throw them *at* anybody, silly. I just want to skip a few. I can make them hop four times at the lake," replied Anthony. "Look at these nice flat ones I found just now in the park."

"They really do look good. I'll bet they would skip perfectly, but remember what Mrs. White said. Even if you don't aim at anybody, on a crowded playground somebody could get hit," reminded Scott.

Just then both boys were startled by the sound of the bell. It rang out across the playground to signal the end of recess. Children everywhere began walking toward the school. As the playground began to clear, Scott got an idea.

"What do you say we skip a few now, Anthony. Nobody can get hurt. Look, everyone has gone inside. Let one go! You try first. Then I'll try just one."

Anthony sent his stone skimming over the playground. It didn't skip, but soared over the ground before coming to rest near the baseball diamond.

"Your turn, Scott, and hurry or we'll be late for class," shouted Anthony.

Scott drew his arm back and let his rock go with as much force as he could. The rock flew out of his hand. It didn't skip as he expected it to. With a crack it hit the brick wall of the school, bounced sideways, and — what was that?

"Oh, no, Scott! Your rock hit the window in the door!" shouted Anthony. "Look at that big crack all the way up to the top! Let's get out of here. No one will know it was you and I. Let's go!"

Scott stood there looking at the window with its big ugly crack. What should he do?

Billy's Award

"Promise you won't tell! Promise!"

"All right, I promise. Cross my heart."

"Good. Now here's what I want you to do." Billy was serious as he spoke to his younger brother, Mark. "Tell the bus driver I'm not going to school

today. Say good-by to Dad and don't stop to talk."

Mark looked worried. "I wish you weren't running away," he said. "Which way are you going?"

"Over the south hill. I'll hitch a ride to one of those big cattle ranches and get a job looking after calves. I'll be okay. When I'm rich I'll come home and help Dad build a new barn. Now scram!"

Through the window they saw the big yellow Alberta school bus slowing down to a stop at the gate. Mark clattered down the stairs. He shouted "Good-by!" over the droning of the vacuum cleaner.

Billy watched as his brother climbed into the bus. The door closed and the bus drove away. Billy sighed with relief. The first part of his plan had worked. Mark was a great kid but next year they would be in the same grade if Billy failed his reading again. The thought was unbearable to Billy.

He tiptoed into the closet and sat on the floor. The next part was waiting until his dad had gone off to the early morning meeting about the August Fair. Billy felt sad because he wouldn't be able to show his calf. This was Billy's first year in 4-H and Bub was a good calf.

Downstairs the vacuum cleaner droned to a stop. Billy heard the sound of footsteps tumbling over one another as his dad rushed up the stairs. Then the sound stopped at the bedroom door. Billy held his breath.

Billy had made the bed. Were *all* the clothes hung up? The footsteps moved away. Billy breathed again. Soon he heard his dad leaving. The kitchen door slammed. Finally Billy heard the sound he was waiting for — the roar of the truck starting.

He ran to the window and waited until the old, red truck disappeared along the road to town. "I'll buy him a new one when I get back," he promised.

In a hurry now, he rolled his quilt into a bundle and tied it with binder twine. With it he ran down to the kitchen. He grabbed some cans off the shelf and threw them into a large, green garbage bag. Half a loaf of bread and a tub of margarine followed the cans. The boy twisted the top of the bag into a knot and heaved it onto his shoulder. He tucked his bundle under his arm and headed for the barn for a last good-by to his precious calf.

"Mark will take good care of you," he whispered to Bub. He was rewarded with a moist lick. Bub returned to his feeding.

Billy wrinkled his freckled nose as he left the barn. There was an odd smell in the barn. It wasn't a good barn smell. Billy forgot about it as he started to climb the south hill.

His straight, brown hair was sticking to his forehead in moist clumps by the time he reached the top of the hill. He was glad to put down his heavy packages and stop for a rest. He looked down at the square, two-story house that had been home for all of his nine years. It looked lonely. The old barn was sway-backed, like the mare he and Mark used to ride. Wait! Wasn't that a little curl of smoke swirling out from the hayloft end of the barn?

Billy couldn't believe his eyes! Then he remembered the funny smell. Cigarette smoke. How could that be? Bub! Bub was in there! That thought sent Billy racing down the hill.

The barn was full of smoke. Billy got Bub out of the barn. He put him into the little corral. Luckily the wind was blowing the smoke away from the corral, not toward it. The animals in the corral would not be harmed.

Billy dashed back into the barn to see what else he could save. He heard a moaning sound. Of course! Cigarette smoke meant someone had slept in the barn.

The smoke made Billy's eyes sting. Coughing and choking, he groped his way toward the smoldering hay. A man lay there in a crumpled heap.

Tears were streaming from Billy's eyes. He grabbed the man by the arms and dragged him along the floor. After what seemed hours they reached the door and fresh air.

33

Panting, Billy drew in gulps of fresh air. He began to feel better. The man on the ground stirred. He sat up, rubbing his eyes. He caught sight of the tiny lick of flame at the top of the barn.

"Wow!" he cried as he leaped to his feet. The man was wide awake now. He was only about a head and a half taller than Billy. "What's going on here?"

"Your cigarette set the barn on fire," replied Billy.

"Oh no!" exclaimed the man. "You're right. I did light one. I must have fallen asleep again. You saved my life. You'd better phone for help. I'll get

some water."

Billy's face turned red. He did not move.

"What's the matter? You do have a phone, don't you?"

"Yes, but I can't read," blurted out the boy.

"In that case I'll go with you," said the man briskly. Just as they reached the house, they heard a loud S-Swoosh as smoke burst into flame. They phoned the fire chief, found some pails, and raced to the pump by the corral. Flames crackled and snapped. Black smoke hissed out of the cracks. Bits of wood splintered off the barn and cinders flew in all directions.

They threw pail after pail of water on the sizzling building. Soon their faces were streaked with soot and sweat. As they pumped and carried the water, the man talked to Billy.

"My name is Bill," he said. "What's yours?"

"Same as yours — but they call me Billy. Are you running away from home, too?"

"Something like that. Why? Were *you* running away?" The man smiled in such a friendly way that suddenly Billy was telling him the whole story.

He shouted it out in short bursts of words because they were pumping and hurrying to the barn and throwing the water at the same time.

"I just can't get the hang of reading. The teacher says I might have to do this year over again. I wouldn't mind, only Mark — that's my brother — would be in my class. I couldn't stand that. I was running away. When I saw the smoke, I had to come back."

"I'm glad you did," said Bill. "Don't worry. We'll work something out. I caused this mess. I'll have to do something about it. You are a fine person. You didn't panic and you remembered to do all the right things. That is just as important as reading. I just bet you can handle reading too."

Billy felt better right away. By the time the fire-fighters came with his dad, the fire was almost out. Everyone set to work to finish the job.

Later over coffee and food for Bill and milk for Billy, Billy's dad heard both stories.

"The whole thing was my fault," explained Bill. "I'd been sick and was hiking across the province to get back in shape. I couldn't find a place to stay for the night. It was very late when I got to the barn. I was going to explain this morning. Billy has saved my life."

"That's all very well," said Billy's dad, "but what am I going to do about my barn?"

"Let me rebuild your barn," replied Bill. "I have some experience as a carpenter."

Billy's dad looked doubtful. "I couldn't pay you anything."

Bill laughed. "Some of this good cooking would suit me fine. Billy can help me and, in return, I'll work with him on his reading. How's that?"

It was settled. When they spoke to Billy's teacher he promised to wait until September before deciding about Billy's reading.

All summer Bill and Billy worked hard. They talked and read; they hammered and nailed. One day the barn was finished; another day the words on the page came alive for Billy. In between times, Billy fed and groomed Bub.

At last the day of the August Fair arrived. Billy saw his teacher at the fair. "I can read now," Billy told him proudly.

At the fair there were two surprises for Billy. First Bub won a Blue Ribbon. "Hurray for Bub!" shouted Billy. Then Billy got an award for bravery. "Hurray for Billy!" shouted the crowd. People came up to shake Billy's hand.

"How does it feel to be a hero?" asked the *Times* reporter.

"I feel about ten feet tall," replied Billy, beaming. "But it sure is hard on the hands."

The Sun

Every day coming,
every day going,
bringing a goldness
out of the black,

Every day climbing
over the heavens,
sinking at sunset,
soon to be back,

42

Coming and going,
going and coming,
leaving no footprint,
leaving no track.

Aileen Fisher

43

The Tall Grass Zoo

This is the Tall Grass Zoo.

It has no camels from the hot desert,
No tigers from the jungle,
No lions from deepest Africa,
No cages, no fences, no keepers.

In the Tall Grass Zoo
You can touch all the animals.
You can lift them up.
You can hold them carefully in your hand.
You can examine them carefully with a magnifying glass
Before you put them gently down
To scurry away among the leaves and grass.

The Tall Grass Zoo is your own backyard.

Here is a whole new world for you to explore —
A world full of tiny living things.
So many of them,
There are more than all the people of the earth
Many times over.
Creatures so small
You can stand like a giant over them . . .
A world full of many wonders.
A quiet world, too.
You must stand very still,
Walk very lightly,
Be gentle and kind
To the creatures you find.
You must know where to look
And how to look sharp . . .
Under the leaves,
In the tall, tall grass,
On the bark of trees,
Among the rocks and in the earth.

Let us go and look . . .

45

Exploring the Tall Grass Zoo

Use a magnifying glass to observe creatures of the Tall Grass Zoo. Find out where they live, what they eat, and how they get their food.

Find out how ants travel through grassy areas. Place several stones in their path. What do they do?

Listen for creature sounds. Find the creatures you hear. You could use a tape recorder to tape their sounds.

Find a flowering plant outside and watch to see what creatures come to visit it. Why do these creatures visit the plant?

46

For Digging

For Catching

Find a flowering plant outside and watch to see what creatures come to visit it. Why do these creatures visit the plant?

Catch several creatures. Record the places where you caught them and any problems you may have had trying to catch them.

In your classroom make a home for the creatures that is like their natural home. Each day watch them carefully to see what they do.

Be sure to return them to the Tall Grass Zoo when you have finished studying them.

Rearing cage for caterpillars

For Carrying

47

The Pond

Getting Ready to Visit the Pond

Why are you going to the pond?

What clothes will you wear?

How will you get things ready so that everyone will
have something to do at the pond?

What supplies will you take with you?

For Seeing – Hearing
Tape recorder
Fishscope

For Catching
Broomstick, bent hanger, and net

Kitchen strainers on handles

Tin can on stick

Rubber scoop

At the Pond

Choose some of the following activities to do while you are at the pond.

Make a record of the animals and birds you see at the pond.

Record pond sounds.

Collect different kinds of plant life you see around the pond.

Draw a picture of the pond and the area around it.

Make a fishscope from a cardboard tube to observe the animal life and plant life at the bottom of the pond.

Use a magnifying glass to examine the different kinds of pond life.

Collect some pond life to take back to the classroom.

For Carrying

For Emergency
First aid kit and towel

Net or cloth bag

Before you remove any creatures from the pond, you should know: how to catch them without hurting them or yourself; how to carry them back to the classroom; what you need to make a natural home for them in the classroom

Creature	To Catch	To Carry
Turtle	Net or by hand. Hold upside down so it can't bite!	Pail or strong bag.
Frog or Toad	Strainer, dip net, or by hand.	Net or cloth bag.
Salamander or Newt	As above.	Covered container, a little water.
Fish	Net or strainer.	Pail or covered jar with water.
Crayfish	Strong net or sieve. Not bare hands!	Pail, box, or can. Needs air.
Eggs and Tapoles	Pail or jar. Cover. Have air holes. Don't take many.	Large jar.
Water Insects	Strainer, net, or rubber scoop. Not bare hands!	Net-covered container partly filled with water.

Whirligig beetles

Water scavenger beetle

Back swimmer

50

Water scorpion

Water strider

(plants, dirt, stones, water, etc.); what food to take from the pond or what you must prepare for the pond life to eat.

The chart below gives you some of this information.

To Make a Natural Surrounding	To Feed
Dishpan with stones and an island of moss in the center. A little water and growing plants.	Bits of meat, fish, worms, fruits, vegetables.
Frog, same as turtle, may share home with turtle and snail. Toad, large box with screen, some dry ground, cover.	Bits of fish and worms.
Salamander, same as turtle. Newt, use an aquarium or dishpan and put in water plants.	As above. Place food on straw or toothpick.
Aquarium or large dishpan. Growing plants from pond.	Insects, worms, fish food, fine cereal.
As above. Keep separate. They fight and eat other life.	Bits of fish, meat, plants, worms – every other day.
In separate large jars with water, plants, and pond scum.	Fish food.
Deep pan, shallow water. Don't put large and small together. Pond water, algae, water plants.	Smaller creatures, bits of meat, fish, plants.

Giant water bug

Water boatman

Caddis fly

Great diving water beetle

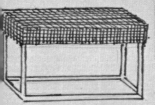

Metal frame tank, screen top

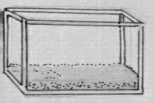

Layer of sand on bottom

Ways to Fill

Pour water on newspaper

A New Home for Your Pond Life

Your pond life needs the same kind of home in the classroom as it had at the pond. You can make a home like this in an aquarium. Study the pictures of the different types of aquariums and decide what type you will make.

Do not use a metal container for your aquarium. Metal could make the water poisonous.

Be sure your aquarium is large enough for your pond life to move around easily and get enough air.

Do not keep large and small meat-eating pond life together. (The large would likely eat the small!)

If you want to cover the aquarium, be sure you leave a space or make holes for air to enter.

Taking Care of Your Pond Life

Remember that the pond life is for you to watch and study. Don't play with them or treat them as pets.

When your study is over, return them to their home.

Pour water in saucer

Stone and stick above water for air-breathing creatures

Remember, after their short stay with you the pond life will be happy to be home again.

Getting to Know Your Pond Life

Watch and record the kinds of foods your pond life eats.

Record the changes you observe in the tadpoles. Do changes take place in any of the other pond life?

Watch how they move, eat, and breathe. Talk with your classmates about the things you observe.

Pretend that you are one of the pond life and write a letter back to the pond telling what has happened to you.

Beyond the Pond

What other things can you think of that need water in order to get around?

What are some ways that we use water?

Choose one of these topics to find out more about. You might like to do your research on one of the following: fish; water birds; flowers around ponds and streams; boats; uses we make of water.

THE MAGIC LISTENING CAP

There once lived an honest old man who was kind and good, but who was so poor he hardly had enough to eat each day. What made him sadder than not having enough to eat himself was that he could no longer bring an offering to his guardian god at the nearby shrine.

"If only I could bring even an offering of fish," he thought sadly.

Finally one day, when his house was empty and he had nothing left to eat, he walked to the shrine of his god. He got on his knees and bowed down before him.

"I've come today to offer the only thing I have left," he said sadly. "I have only myself to offer now. Take my life if you will have it."

The old man knelt silently and waited for the god to speak.

Soon there was a rumbling sound, and the man heard a voice that seemed to come from far, far away.

"Don't worry, old man," the god said to him. "You have been honest and you have been good. From today on I shall change your fortune, and you shall suffer no longer."

Then the guardian god gave the old man a little red cap. "Take this cap, old man," he said. "It is a magic listening cap. With this on your head you will be able to hear such sounds as you have never heard before."

The old man looked up in surprise. He was old, but he heard quite well. He had heard many, many sounds during the long years of his life.

"What do you mean?" he asked his god. "What new sounds are there in this world that I have not yet heard?"

The god smiled. "Have you ever really heard what the nightingale says as it flies to the plum tree in the spring? Have you ever understood what the trees whisper to one another when their leaves rustle in the wind?"

The old man shook his head. He understood. "Thank you," he said. "Thank you for this wonderful gift." Carrying the cap with great care, he hurried toward his home.

As the old man walked along, the sun grew hot. He stopped to rest in the shade of a big tree that stood at the roadside. Suddenly he saw two black crows fly into the tree. One came from the mountains, and the other from the sea. He could hear their noisy chatter fill the air above him. Now was the time to try his magic cap! Quickly he put it on, and as soon as he did, he could understand everything the crows were saying.

"How is life in the land beyond the sea?" asked the mountain crow.

"Ah, life is not easy," answered the crow of the sea. "It grows harder and harder to find food for my young ones. But tell me, did you have any interesting news from the mountains?"

"All is not well in our land either," answered the crow from the mountains. "We are worried about our friend, the camphor tree, who grows weaker and weaker but can neither live nor die."

"Why, how can that be?" asked the crow of the sea.

"It is an interesting tale," answered the mountain crow. "About six years ago a wealthy man in our town built a guest house in his garden. He cut down the camphor tree in order to build the house, but the roots were never dug out. The tree is not dead but neither can it live, for each time it sends out new shoots from beneath the house they are cut off by the gardener."

"Ah, the poor tree," said the crow of the sea sadly. "What will it do?"

"It forever cries and moans, but alas, human beings are very stupid," said the mountain crow. "No one seems to hear it, and it has cast an evil spell on the wealthy man and made him very ill. If they don't dig up the tree and plant it where it can grow, the spell will not be broken and the man will soon die. He has been very ill for a long, long time."

The two crows sat in the tree and talked of many things, but the old man who listened below could not forget the story of the dying man and the camphor tree.

"If only I could save them both," he thought. "I am probably the only human being who knows what is making the man ill."

He got up quickly and all the way home he tried to think of some way to save the dying man. "I could go to his home and tell him exactly what I heard," he thought. "But surely no one will believe me if I say I heard two crows talking in a tree. I must think of a clever way to be heard and believed."

As he walked along a good idea suddenly came to him. "I shall pretend to be a fortune teller," he thought. "Then surely they will believe me."

The very next day the old man took his little red cap and set out for the town where the sick man lived. He walked by the front gate of this man's home, calling in a loud voice, "Fortunes! Fortunes! I tell fortunes!" Soon the gate opened and the sick man's wife came out.

"Come in, old man. Come in," she said. "Tell me how I can make my husband well. I have had doctors from near and far, but they can do nothing for him."

The old man went inside and listened to the woman's story. "We have tried herbs and medicines from many, many lands, but they do not help," she said sadly.

Then the old man said, "Did you not build a guest house in your garden six years ago?" The woman nodded. "And hasn't your husband been ill ever since?"

"Yes," answered the woman, nodding. "That's right. How did you know?"

"A fortune teller knows many things," the old man answered. Then he said, "Let me sleep in your guest house tonight. Tomorrow I shall know how your husband can be cured."

"Yes, of course," she answered. "I shall do anything to cure my husband."

That night after a great feast the old man was taken to the guest house. Beautiful quilts were laid out for him and a charcoal brazier was brought in to keep him warm.

As soon as he was quite alone, the old man put on his red cap and sat quietly, waiting to hear the camphor tree speak. He slid open the paper doors and looked out at the sky sprinkled with glowing stars. He waited and waited, but the night was silent and he didn't even hear the whisper of a sound. As he sat in the darkness, the old man began to wonder if the crows had been wrong.

"Perhaps there is no dying camphor tree after all," he thought. Still wearing his red cap, the old man climbed into the quilts and closed his eyes.

Suddenly he heard a soft rustling sound like many leaves trembling in the wind. Then he heard a low, gentle voice.

"How do you feel tonight, camphor tree?" the voice called into the silence.

Then the old man heard a hollow sound that seemed to come from beneath the floor.

"Ah, is that you, pine tree?" it asked weakly. "I do not feel well at all. I think I am about to die . . . about to die . . ." it moaned softly.

Soon another voice whispered, "It's I, the cedar tree from across the path. Do you feel better tonight, camphor tree?"

One after the other the trees of the garden whispered gently to the camphor tree, asking how it felt. Each time the camphor tree answered weakly, "I am dying . . . I am dying . . ."

The old man knew that if the tree died the master of the house would also die. Early the next morning he hurried to the bedside of the dying man. He told him about the tree and about the evil spell it had cast upon him.

"If you want to live," he said, "have the camphor tree dug up quickly and plant it somewhere in your garden where it can grow."

The sick man nodded weakly. "I will do anything if only I can become well and strong again."

That very morning carpenters and gardeners were called to come from the village. The carpenters tore out the floor of the guest house and found the stump of the camphor tree. Carefully, carefully, the gardeners lifted it out of the earth and then moved it into the garden where it had room to grow. The old man, wearing his red cap, watched as the tree was planted where the moss was green and damp.

"Ah, at last," he heard the camphor tree sigh. "I can reach up again to the good clean air. I can grow once more!"

As soon as the tree was moved, the wealthy man began to grow stronger. Before long he felt so much better he could get up for a few hours each day. Then he was up all day long, and finally he was well again.

"I must thank the old fortune teller for saving my life," he said, "for if he had not come to tell me about the camphor tree, I would probably not be alive today."

The wealthy man sent for the old man with the little red cap.

"You were far wiser than any of the doctors who came from near and far to see me," he said to the old man. Then, giving him many bags filled with gold, he said, "Take this gift and with it my life-long thanks. When this gold is gone, I shall see that you get more."

"Ah, you are indeed very kind," the old man said happily, and taking his gold, he set off for home.

As soon as he got home, he took some of the gold coins and went to the village market. There he bought rice cakes and sweet tangerines and the very best fish he could find. He hurried with them to his guardian god and placed them before the shrine.

"My fortunes have indeed changed since you gave me this wonderful magic cap," the old man said. "I thank you more than I can say."

Each day after that the old man went to the shrine and never forgot to bring an offering of rice or wine or fish to his god. He was able to live in comfort and never had to worry again about not having enough to eat. Because the old man was not greedy, he put away his magic listening cap and didn't try to tell any more fortunes. Instead he lived quietly and happily the rest of his days.

The Mystery of No. 30

Part One

Sal stood looking up and down the street with a frown on his face. His friend Nicola had gone downtown to the dentist, and Sal couldn't think of anything interesting to do. Across the street Jerome and Frank were playing marbles, but that didn't interest him.

Sal pulled down the zipper of his jacket. As he did so his fingers touched a round metal disc pinned to his jacket lining. His face brightened. It was a metal badge and it said, "Detective No. 30." The badge had been one of his birthday presents. He would practice shadowing! He could do that by himself. Now who was there to shadow?

Sal headed up the street. Why not shadow Jerome and Frank! Of course Frank and Jerome mustn't suspect they were being shadowed. Sal crossed the street and hid behind a tree. Carefully he looked out. No, they hadn't noticed him. Darting from tree to tree Sal came closer. If they were up to anything suspicious they'd better look out!

To Sal's disgust Jerome, without even turning his head, said, "Hi, Sal. Want to join us?"

Sal snorted in disgust. Those kids didn't know a detective when they saw one.

Just then he noticed a car parking at the curb and a man, whom he didn't know, getting out of it. This was more like it! He'd bet that man was up to something. Well, he'd better beware of Detective No. 30!

The man started up the street toward the drugstore. Sal stopped once and pretended to tie his shoelace. That way the man wouldn't suspect he was being shadowed. The man entered the drugstore and went into the telephone booth. There the man shut the door. Sal took some money from his pocket and bought some peanuts. If the man noticed him at all, he saw only a boy munching peanuts. He didn't know that that same boy was shadowing him.

The man went to his parked car. Sal thought his shadowing job was finished, but now the man did something strange. He got in and started the motor. Then he got out, leaving the motor running. Looking about, the man walked quickly up the path to the Stones' house and then went around to the back.

Sal was all eyes. Nearby were some large empty crates. Sal crept into one of them. Through the cracks he could see both the house and the car. The license plate was bent and at first Sal could hardly read it. Finally he wrote the number down. Wasn't that man ever coming out?

Now the front door was opening! Sal watched carefully. It wasn't the man he was trailing after all! That man had a smooth face with a big nose. This man had a fuzzy gray beard, wore a gray hat, and was carrying a suitcase. Just then the man passed close to Sal's hiding place. Sal gave such a loud gasp of surprise that the man would have heard him if he hadn't been in such a hurry. He rushed over to the parked car, jumped in, and sped away.

Sal, eyes and mouth wide open, came out of the crate and stood watching. Just then he heard, "Hi, Sal!" It was Nicola. "Hey, there's a great movie playing downtown," Nicola gasped, all out of breath. Nicola was almost always in a hurry. "It's a funny movie! All about a little car that goes forward, backward and upside-down all by itself! Want to see it Saturday?" Sal got so interested in the movie that he forgot to tell Nicola about his adventure.

Part Two

At breakfast the next morning Sal was very quiet. He was thinking of some way of asking his mother for his allowance early. He usually got his allowance on Sunday but the movie would be in town only until Saturday.

Sal's mother was reading the paper. She turned to Sal, "The Stones' house over in the next block was broken into yesterday while the Stones were away. A lot of silver was taken. The thieves seem to have carried the loot away in a stolen suitcase. There aren't any clues and the Stones are offering a reward."

Sal laid down his spoon. "Would the reward be big enough so I could go to the movie on Saturday?"

"Do *you* know something about this robbery, Sal?" asked Sal's mother.

Sal told his mother how he had seen the man with the big nose go into the Stones' house. Right away Sal's mother called the police station.

In a short time a car stopped in front of the house, and a police officer came into the house.

"Are you the boy who can help us catch this thief?" asked the officer. "Tell me everything you saw." Again Sal told his story.

"Did you write down the license number of the car?" asked the officer.

"Yes," answered Sal, "I thought a real detective would." Sal fished a crumpled piece of paper from his pocket. Sure enough, there was the number.

"You've done some good detective work," said the police officer as he was writing in his notebook. "It won't be hard now to pick up that car. If we find it, we'd like you to come down to the station to see if you can identify the thief."

The police officer hurried away. Sal could see Nicola across the street. He called to her, "Say, Nicola, when I go down to the police station, want to go with me? Maybe with the reward money I can go to the movie."

Part Three

On Saturday morning Sal and Nicola played close to Sal's house so that they wouldn't miss the call from the police. Around noon Sal's mother called out to them, "The police have a suspect. They think it may be the big-nosed man, and they'd like you to come down to the station to identify him."

When Nicola and Sal reached the station they saw the sergeant sitting behind a large desk. Standing near her desk were a group of men.

Sergeant Degeer spoke first. "Which one of you is the detective?" she asked.

"We both are," answered Nicola, "that is, not real ones, of course, but play ones. Sal is No. 30, and I'm No. 18. It was Sal yesterday."

"Well, Sal," said the sergeant, "the officers have told me what you did yesterday. Now look at those men and see if the man you shadowed yesterday is there."

"Sure he is," answered Sal. "It's that fellow with the big nose."

"So that's the one you followed, is it? But you said the man who came out of the house had a gray beard and a gray cap."

"Yes, he did, but it's the same man," said Sal.

"How can you tell?"

Suddenly Sal grew shy. "You tell her, Nicola."

Nicola pulled her hand from her pocket and showed some small blue stickers. "You see, it's this way. We try to see how many people we can shadow. The one who shadows the most in a certain time wins. But we didn't think it was fair just to follow someone a little way and call that shadowing, so I have these blue stickers, and Sal has red ones. Before we can finish shadowing anyone, we have to get near enough to put one of these stickers on the person. That's what Sal did when he crowded up against the man in the drugstore."

"There's a new idea in shadowing for you!" said Sergeant Degeer. Sal noticed that the big-nosed man looked as if he'd like to get away.

"What happened then?" asked the sergeant, very interested.

Sal took up the story. "I thought it was a different man, too, coming out the front door. But when he passed by me to go back to his car, I saw that red sticker just back of his coat pocket where I'd put it. Maybe it's still there." Sal and Nicola ran over to the big-nosed man. "There it is!" exclaimed Nicola.

"The kids seem to have pinned it on you, all right. You may as well tell us where the loot is. It may help you if you do," said the sergeant.

"Sure, they've caught me," growled big nose, "but you cops wouldn't have got me without the kids. They've got brains."

Just then a gray-haired man who had been listening but saying nothing stepped forward. It was Mr. Stone.

"I'm proud to have you as a neighbor, Sal," he said. "Here's the reward money. Fifty dollars."

"Fifty dollars! Wow! Now I can see that movie for sure! We'd better get going. Are you ready, No. 18?"

Nicola was already at the door. "Ready, No. 30!"

To the Teacher

The Secret Life of Mr. Mugs, the third book of Level Seven in the *Starting Points in Language Arts Program,* introduces 51 New Words to the children. Considered as known words are variants of words taught at Levels One through Six formed by adding *s, es, 's, ed,* and *ing;* by dropping the silent *e* ending to add *ed* or *ing;* by doubling the final consonant to add *ed* or *ing.* All words with phonetic and structural elements taught in Levels One through Five are considered as known words. Also considered as known are words formed by combining known words into compounds. Words that are new to the program, but contain phonemic and structural elements previously taught are considered as Decodable Words; these words are not listed here, but appear in the Teacher's Guide. Some words that are known or Decodable, but whose meaning cannot readily be understood in context, are included under New Words. The New Words are listed here in the order of their appearance in the book. Starred words are included for enrichment purposes.

Page

6. catnip
7. . . . . . .
8. hearty
   warehouses
9. . . . . . .
10. ached
11. . . . . . .
12. . . . . . .
13. doubtfully
14. . . . . . .

---

16. cough
    sofa cushion*
    cure
17. . . . . . .
18. allowance
19. cavities*
20. comforting
21. . . . . . .
22. tangerines
23. ballet
    twitchy*
    gnawing*
24. period*
25. . . . . . .

---

28. award

29. hitch
    calves
    droning
    vacuum cleaner
    sighed
    unbearable
30. August Fair
31. 4 – H*
    binder twine*
    margarine*
    moist
    sway-backed*
    mare*
32. . . . . . .
33. groped
    smoldering*
34. . . . . . .
35. blurted
    splintered*
    cinders
    soot*
36. . . . . . .
37. experience
38. groomed*
    beaming*

---

44. magnifying glass
45. . . . . . .

46. observe
    areas
47. natural

---

48. supplies
49. activities
50. salamander
    newt
    container
    crayfish
51. aquarium
    separate
    pond scum*
    algae
52. . . . . . .
53. topics*
    research*

---

54. honest
    offering
    guardian god
    shrine
55. . . . . . .
56. nightingale*
    rustle
57. camphor tree
58. evil spell
59. . . . . . .

60. herbs*
    charcoal brazier*
61. . . . . . .
62. . . . . . .
63. . . . . . .
64. . . . . . .
_____
66. mystery

No.
disc*
shadowing
suspicious*
67. . . . . . .
68. . . . . . .
69. . . . . . .
70. license

71. movie
72. . . . . . .
73. identify
74. Sergeant Degeer
75. . . . . . .
76. . . . . . .
77. . . . . . .
78. . . . . . .

CDEFG 079